FAR OUT
FABLES

raintree

a Capstone company — publishers for children

INTRODUCING...

COMPETITOR 1:
SHELLY THE TORTOISE

ROBOT:
MEGA TORTOISE

STATS:
ATTACK: 6
DEFENCE: 9
SPEED: 1

SPECIAL:
Tough armoured shell
Hidden power tools

COMPETITOR 2:
HUNTER THE HARE

ROBOT:
HAZARD HARE

STATS:
ATTACK: 7
DEFENCE: 2
SPEED: 10

SPECIAL:
Destructive laser eyes
Hammer arm

COMPETITOR 3:
FOREST THE SQUIRREL

ROBOT:
NUTTY DESTROYER

STATS:
ATTACK: 7
DEFENCE: 4
SPEED: 3

COMPETITOR 4:
ROSIE THE PORCUPINE

ROBOT:
SHARP SHOOTER

STATS:
ATTACK: 5
DEFENCE: 8
SPEED: 5

COMPETITOR 5:
JAY THE BIRD

ROBOT:
BEAK OF FURY

STATS:
ATTACK: 6
DEFENCE: 5
SPEED: 8

COMPETITOR 6:
MARTIN THE MOUSE

ROBOT:
MUTANT MONSTER

STATS:
ATTACK: 3
DEFENCE: 2
SPEED: 5

COMPETITOR 7:
DORA THE DOE

ROBOT:
DEER THE ROBOT SLAYER

STATS:
ATTACK: 9
DEFENCE: 7
SPEED: 5

Raintree is an imprint of Capstone Global Library Limited, a company Incorporated in England and Wales having its registered office at 264 Banbury Road, Oxford, OX2 7DY – Registered company number: 6695582

www.raintree.co.uk
myorders@raintree.co.uk

Designed by Hilary Wacholz
Edited by Abby Huff
Lettered by Jaymes Reed

ISBN 978 1 474 75030 1
21 20 19 18 17
10 9 8 7 6 5 4 3 2 1

British Library Cataloguing in Publication Data: A full catalogue record for this book is available from the British Library.

Printed and bound in china

FAR OUT FABLES

THE ROBO-BATTLE OF MEGA TORTOISE VS HAZARD HARE

A GRAPHIC NOVEL

BY STEPHANIE PETERS
ILLUSTRATED BY FERNANDO CANO

In the spring, the forest was beautiful. The sun shone. The trees rustled in the warm breezes. It was a quiet, peaceful time . . .

Except for the week of the annual Spring Fair!

The Spring Fair always ended with a spectacular competition. Each year was different.

But no matter what the event was . . .

BOING

Ooooo!

Every year . . .

Splat

Splat

Aaaahh!

Hunter the Hare came in first.

You call this a challenge? *Please!*

7

The following year, the Spring Fair announced a new competition.

ROBOT BATTLE!

BUILD! BATTLE! WIN!

LAST ONE STANDING TAKES FIRST PRIZE!

A robot battle?! *Epic!*

Prepare to be *crushed.*

Meanwhile, in Shelly's workshop . . .

OK, let's think. Hunter always wins. So what if I make a robo-suit that can do everything Hunter does?

SLOW AND STEADY

zzzzz

It has to bounce really *high* and be *super fast*. Ooo, and it has to have a *nasty stare!*

Shelly worked through the night.

By sunrise, she had her design.

Now, to *build* it!

She spent all day hammering, sawing and welding.

WHAM BANG
WHAM
WHAM
ZZZTT
ZZZTT

13

By nightfall, she had her prototype.

Ta-da, just like Hunter! Is this robo-suit a winner or what?

Um...

That night, other animals were at the fair having fun.

But Shelly was still hard at work.

Here goes *nothing!*

OK, time to test it out.

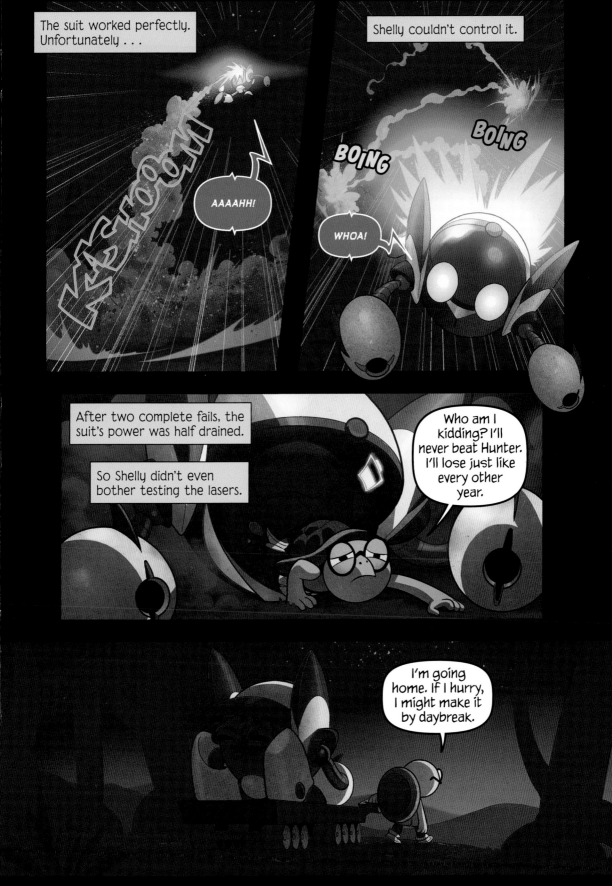

Hunter didn't see Shelly, but he *did* see her robo-suit.

Well, well. What have we here?

Finders keepers, losers... well, I don't know *anything* about losers. *Ha!*

All my hard work – I can't believe he just *took* it!

Oh, wait. *Yes, I can.* It's Hunter, after all. He doesn't understand hard work because he never works *hard.*

You know what? I'm *not* giving up. I'm back in it.

And I'm going to *win!*

With three days left until the robo-battle, Shelly got to work.

Trying to be Hunter was a *big mistake.* I have to be *me.*

Go! Go!

I'm good at hiding.

So what if I'm slow and steady? That can be a good thing, right?

And if Hunter uses my *first* suit...

Well, I know its strengths and its *weakness.*

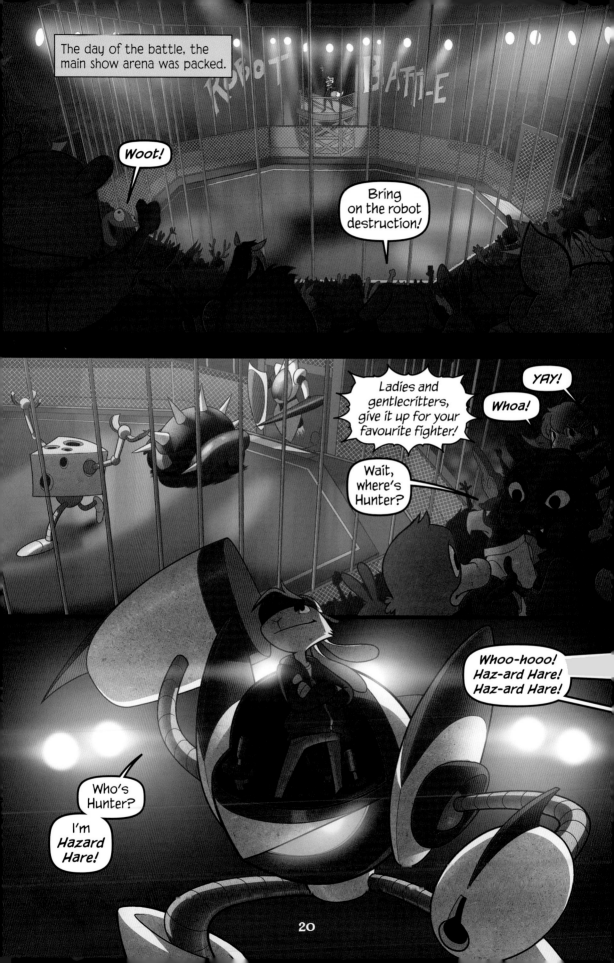

No one noticed the last competitor enter the arena.

OK, Shelly. Time to show 'em what you're made of!

Are you ready for extreme *smashing* and *mashing?!*

Many will enter the arena, but only two will survive for the *final* face-off.

The last one standing will be crowned...the *ULTIMATE ROBO-CHAMPION!*

The lights went out. A hush fell over the crowd. Then a horn blasted . . .

WHAAWAA

In the chaos, no one noticed Shelly.

WHAT? HEY!

Which is just what she had planned.

Take them out one at a time.

KACHUNG

AH!

SURPRISE!

BONK

AW, NUTS!

25

AND YOU'RE A BORN LOSER!

Is this it for Mega Tortoise?

ZZZZTTT

SMACK

Activate mirror shield!

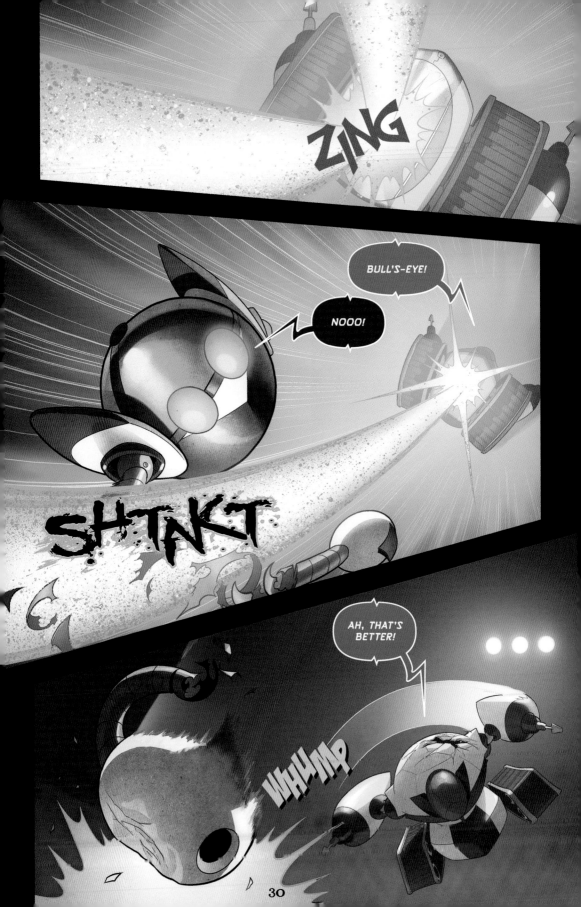

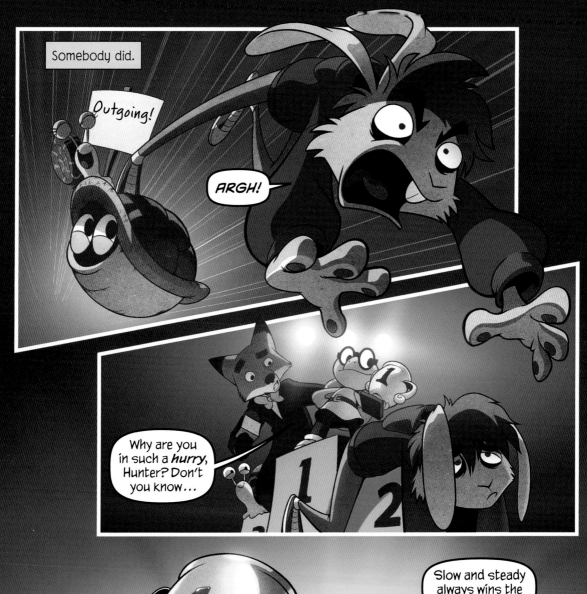

Somebody did.

Outgoing!

ARGH!

Why are you in such a *hurry*, Hunter? Don't you know...

Slow and steady always wins the *robo-battle!*

33

ALL ABOUT FABLES

A fable is a short tale that teaches the reader a lesson about life, often with animal characters. Most fables were first told thousands of years ago by a Greek storyteller called Aesop. At the end of a fable, there's almost always a moral (a fancy word for lesson) stated very clearly, so you don't miss it. Yes, fables can be a bit bossy, but they usually give pretty good advice. Read on to learn more about Aesop's original fable and its moral. Can you spot any other lessons?

THE TORTOISE AND THE HARE

One day, a hare makes fun of a tortoise's legs. "Your legs are so stubby! Mine are much faster and stronger," Hare boasts. Tortoise isn't impressed. "I bet I could beat you in a race," he says. Hare laughs at the thought of Tortoise winning, but he accepts the challenge. A fox agrees to judge their competition. Tortoise and Hare take their marks. Then they're off! Hare speeds down the path. He's so confident he will win that halfway through the race, he lies down and takes a nap. *I can rest and still run laps around Tortoise!* Hare thinks as he drifts off to sleep. Meanwhile, Tortoise plods forward step by step. When Hare wakes up from his snooze, he dashes to the finish line. But he's too late. Tortoise has already crossed the line and won!

THE MORAL

SLOW AND STEADY WINS THE RACE
(In other words, don't be lazy –
you have to work hard
to reach your goals!)

A **FAR OUT** GUIDE TO THE FABLE'S ROBO TWISTS!

We don't know much about the tortoise in Aesop's version. Here Shelly is a smart girl who's into engineering and technology.

In the original fable, Tortoise challenges Hare to a race. In this story, Shelly vows to defeat Hunter in an epic robot battle!

Hunter doesn't take a nap in this far-out version, but he does mess about when he should be building a robot suit.

Tortoise steadily walks to the finish line in the original. Shelly slowly takes apart Hunter's suit and keeps her calm to take first prize!

VISUAL QUESTIONS

In graphic novels, you can learn a lot about characters just through the art. Look back at page 12 and 13. Compare and contrast Hunter's home and Shelly's workshop. What does the art tell you about each animal?

After two complete fails, the suit's power was half drained.

So Shelly didn't even bother testing the lasers.

Who am I kidding? I'll never beat Hunter. I'll lose just like every other year.

Foreshadowing is a clue about something that will happen later in the story. After Shelly tests her first suit, we see the half-empty battery indicator. What event is the art foreshadowing?
(Hint: Think about how Hunter loses the battle.)

How does Hunter feel going into the battle? Use examples from the text and art to support your answer.

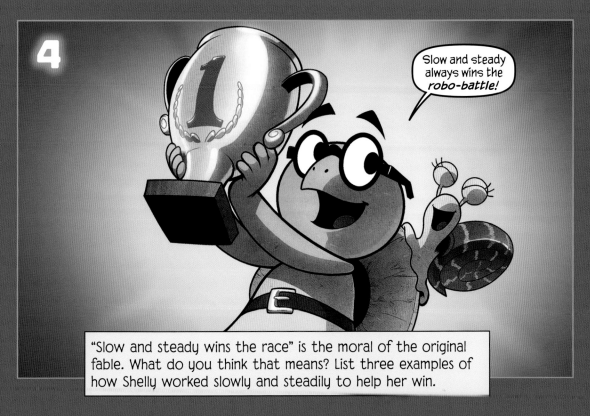

"Slow and steady wins the race" is the moral of the original fable. What do you think that means? List three examples of how Shelly worked slowly and steadily to help her win.

AUTHOR

Stephanie Peters worked as a children's book editor for ten years before she started writing books herself. She has since written forty books, including *Sleeping Beauty*, *Magic Master* and the New York Times best seller *A Princess Primer: A Fairy Godmother's Guide to Being a Princess*. When not at her computer, Peters enjoys playing with her two children, going to the gym or working on home improvement projects with her patient and supportive husband, Daniel.

ILLUSTRATOR

Fernando Cano is an illustrator born in Mexico City, Mexico. He currently resides in Monterrey, Mexico, where he makes a living as an illustrator and colourist. He has done work for Marvel, DC Comics and role-playing games like *Pathfinder* from Paizo Publishing. In his spare time, he enjoys hanging out with friends, singing, rowing and drawing!

GLOSSARY

activate turn on or make active

arena large area that is used for sports or entertainment (or robot battles!)

bolt metal rod used to join objects together

champion person who has defeated all others in a competition

chaos total confusion

competition contest between two or more people

disarm take away a person's weapons or their ability to fight

drain empty or use up by small amounts

melee disorderly and confusing fight between lots of people

prototype first version of an invention that tests an idea to see if it will work

repair make something work again; fix

steady a steady person doesn't change much and keeps on going; they are dependable and trustworthy

THE MORAL OF THE STORY IS... EPIC!

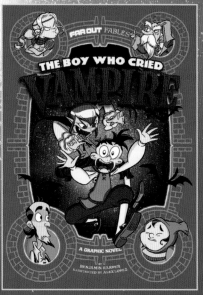

FAR OUT FABLES